Biorhythm
Through Life:
Laxmi's Journey

AF094321

Bomma Latashree

BLUEROSE PUBLISHERS
India | U.K.

Copyright © Bomma Latashree 2025

All rights reserved by author. No part of this publication may be reproduced, stored in a retrieval system or transmitted in any form or by any means, electronic, mechanical, photocopying, recording or otherwise, without the prior permission of the author. Although every precaution has been taken to verify the accuracy of the information contained herein, the publisher assumes no responsibility for any errors or omissions. No liability is assumed for damages that may result from the use of information contained within.

BlueRose Publishers takes no responsibility for any damages, losses, or liabilities that may arise from the use or misuse of the information, products, or services provided in this publication.

For permissions requests or inquiries regarding this publication, please contact:

BLUEROSE PUBLISHERS
www.BlueRoseONE.com
info@bluerosepublishers.com
+91 8882 898 898
+4407342408967

ISBN: 978-93-6783-119-9

Cover Design: Aman Sharma
Typesetting: Pooja Sharma

First Edition: February 2025

Author's Note

Thank you for picking this book up. This book would demand some precious time of yours. The book is compiled of small stories, which the character lives through me as, I wanted to create lot of different imaginations while reading the book and get implied in regular lifestyle.

Use imagination for happiness. It has no limit, limitless…. as sky is the limit. One's inner desires and vivid thoughts create imagination. It's a very important power humans possess - one can emote emotions. Which one should practice in our everyday lives. Imagination is dangerous too as its kind of double edge sword. You need a lot of experience to know how to control the racing mind. Life is fun when one is equipped to enjoy the experience.

As an author this is my first book, hoping to touch the sensitivities of a reader, create that full-fledge experience of reading a book. I have curated this book on lifestyle, hoping you enjoy reading the book. .

Contact: +91 7300022270

About the Author

I'm Bomma Latashree. I have graduated as an Electronic Engineer. As I got married into a business family, could not explore into the field of jobs. I'm a person of varied interest. My first project was in association with NIIT, which franchise I had taken to run multimedia CBSE curriculum based computer courses called LEDA FAMILY CLUB. After which I conceived, had two wonderful boys. Raising my boys was kind of full time occupation for a while which I enjoyed thoroughly. I'm dealer for HINDUSTAN PETROLEUM, they coined me as PROPRETRIX for the business. I have organised couple of SUMMER CAMPS for children, as I could spend more time with my kids in their growing up age. I also ventured into fashion business, opening my own fashion boutique in the prime area of the city called LASH STUDIO. Currently I'm pursuing to be an INFLUENCER on social media. Never thought I would someday write a novel. One of my family member convinced me to publish my own book. I'm very close to him…. he has been the inspiration and motivator in this project.

Contents

Chapter 1: Introduction of character Laxmi 1

Chapter 2: Animal Experience 9

Chapter 3: Road Travel 18

Chapter 4: Bus Ride 28

Chapter 5: Spirituality 33

Chapter 6: Music 42

Chapter 7: Bike Accident 52

Chapter 8: High School 61

Chapter 9: Mela (fete) 70

Chapter 10: Parade 76

Chapter 1

Introduction of character Laxmi

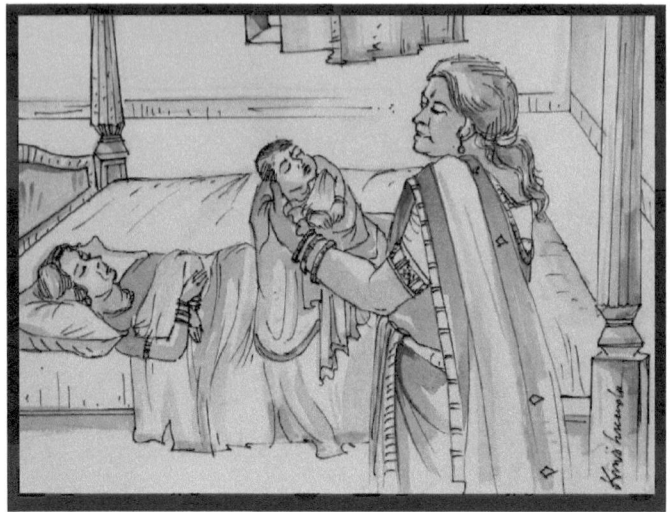

After ages a girl child was born in the family. They considered her as the God's gift, as they were blessed with Lakshmi after many years. For generations only male child was being born in the family. The baby's entry into the world was quite interesting. She entered the world in the middle of the night when the whole world was sleeping and woke up the entire village, announcing her arrival.

The story mainly depicts this baby girl in whole, who came into this world like the rest of us, with lots of dreams and desires of achievement. She was a small bundle of joy, which arrived in a small size with large, beautiful eyes, announcing her arrival with a loud cry.

A rather funny incident occurred at the time of her birth. It was a dark midnight when baby's mother went into labor. Wasting no time, baby's grandmother (maternal) woke her son up, a young teenaged boy to fetch the nurse from her house. She informed the boy that she already had put a word and that she would accompany him immediately. Phones were not that common in those days and so people had to get things done quite personally. The boy, immediately took his cycle out and raced towards the nurse's house. As he reached the house, he hurriedly hit the door to wake them up. Her husband opened the door. The boy narrated the emergency of the situation. Hearing him speak, the nurse came out prepared and instructed the boy to go along first and get the hot water ready assuring that she would reach there with her husband. While heading back in the pitch-dark night mid of the way the boy felt something pulling the cycle from back and not letting him move forward. He imagined all kinds of nasty things that could possibly happen and felt frightened to death in that situation. Finally, as it was getting rather late and since he was assigned such an important task wherein he had to reach home soon, thinking would that be possible now? In village the area was famous for notorious incidents, however as it was the shortest route he opted for it. Offering a silent prayer to God, he eventually summoned enough courage to turn around and face what he assumed to be demons who must have been restricting his movements. In between, he had imagined all forms of demons, he was about to encounter, all the while planning how to outrun them. It was very humid, though it had drizzled a little some while ago. He was sweating like hell, his shirt soaking wet. The sweet scent of petrichor laced the ground.. Slowly as he turned back shivering, ready to face the demon in pitch dark, he merely saw two big bright eyes looking back at him from the darkness. . A strained scream left his mouth. After squinting at the darkness a little more than usual, he saw two rains drops on the leaf of the tree on which moonlight was dancing and he realized that he had imagined something else altogether. When he further looked down, he noticed that a branch had fallen from the tree, stopping him from moving forward. He sighed in relief, hurriedly removing the branch from obstructing his way and zoomed towards the house. As he reached, he saw a couple of the neighbors were around, helping his mother. Before he or the nurse could reach the baby, it had made its entry into the world known to the unprepared family. They all welcomed her with joy and with a lot of patience as they waited for the nurse holding the baby in their hand. Nurse arrived and made everybody leave from the room, for doing the needful. It was an epic entry of the baby girl into the world.

The next day was sunny and the sun came out shining brightly. Before everybody else, the baby woke up with a loud cry, waking up the whole house. As last night was long and tiring, they had all overslept in the morning. Mother fed the baby till her stomach was full and put the baby back to sleep. Before the baby could wake up again, the household started its preparation in welcoming the baby as they could not follow the rituals in mid of the previous night. About an hour's sleep later, the baby woke up again.

Firstly, the elders in the family took away the bad omen (nazar) by rotating a big plate three times containing water mixed up with turmeric and quick lime (Chuna) which turned the water red. After the rounds, the water was thrown away. Then, the baby was taken to the bath, wherein special ladies were assigned to do the job. The way they handled the baby, it was evident that they were experienced. To start with, the lady gave a through massage with hot oil in a traditional and practiced manner. Then body powder (ubtan) was applied to the whole body and finally she was bathed with the steaming hot water. After the bath, the baby was treated to benzoin smoke (sambrani), for the whole body and especially her hair so it could dry her hair which were thick black. The baby was wrapped nicely in a thick cloth and handed over to the mother. All this took more than an hour to finish and by the end of it, the baby was too tired and hungry. As soon she was fed, she dozed off in no time. The baby and her mother stayed at the maternal grandparent's home for three months after the delivery until the mother could recover and handle the baby, solely by herself.

The day arrived when the baby was to leave for her home. Baby's father along with her paternal grandparents had visited to take the baby and the mother home.

The baby girl was bestowed with the name Lakshmi, as she had bought a lot of happiness and prosperity into the family. When the baby was taken home, she was welcomed by lighting camphor on pumpkin. Later, a pooja was performed which was followed by a lunch for guests. Her arrival was considered auspicious as her father got promoted to a higher position and posted to a bigger city after her birth.

Lakshmi started her schooling (kinder garden) in that new city. Her school was located just at the backyard of their house and she loved spending her time there. She had an amazing childhood as her grandparents stayed along with them, which turned out to be a great support system. It was a small nuclear family with four kids, parents and grandparents.

Weekdays were always busy and spent hustling. It was only on the weekends that they got time to spend together as a family. Most of the time either some friends were visiting them or they were visiting close friends and nearby families and spending time together. Even shopping was planned on weekends itself. Among all the siblings, Lakshmi was the closest to her father, and he too, pampered her a lot. They even nicknamed her DB (Daddy's Beti). Though all the kids were raised & pampered equally, all of them felt that a little partiality was being bestowed towards Lakshmi, which she enjoyed thoroughly and took advantage of. The privilege was used by her when needed.

One day on a shopping date, Lakshmi saw a beautiful doll and wanted to purchase it to play with it. As she was very young to understand the logistics, she simply showed her father the doll so that he could buy the doll for her. With a lot of enthusiasm both Lakshmi and her father picked the doll and took it to the counter. The sales person showed the price tag to her father. Looking at the price Lakshmi's father turned towards her with a little hesitation and promised that he'll buy that doll later and asking her to pick something else for now. In That instant, the sweet little girl turned into an adamant naughty girl and insisted on buying the same doll. She displayed all her tantrums, crying and running out of the shop to sit right in middle of the road, jamming the traffic from both the sides. As Lakshmi's father tried to pick her up, she again slipped under his hands and started rolling on the road, creating a big scene there by putting the whole family in an embarrassed state. Still, her father didn't budge on buying the doll and rather bought some ice cream and returned home.

The next day everyone got busy with their work, forgetting about the previous night and resumed the day ahead. By evening, when everybody was home and settling in for the night, Lakshmi's father walked in returning from the office.

After entering, he called out for Lakshmi, and she went running to her father. While running, she saw her father was holding something in his hands. To her surprise it was the same doll for which she had created that nuisance. He then put the doll in Lakshmi's hand and kissed her on the forehead.

When Lakshmi grew older, her father shared that incident with her and told her that he was falling short of money then so he needed some time. It was a lesson in understanding the situation and having some patience and maturity.

She passed that year and went to the next class of kinder garden. She was an intelligent kid and scored good marks in school. Now that they were comfortable, and had gotten accustomed to their surroundings, just then another career opening came to Lakshmi's father. It was a big promotion but this time it was located in a remote area, where a big project was being executed and he had to head a department all by himself. With the kids growing up and the place being remote, Lakshmi's father was a little hesitant to agree to the offer. . The management convinced him by promising a good career growth along with quality education for the kids. That encouraged her father to go ahead, and take the step to move the whole family to the remote location with fewer amenities than the city offered. He accepted the job offer as the kids were still young and could not understand the difference in places.. The project was at a very early stage, where the land was still being procured for the project. For officers, there were six quarters along with a Guesthouse constructed and that was it. No proper electricity, water or other amenities were available and there was dense forest all around, along with some agricultural land in between. Lot of insects & worms would crawl in the night around the lights, so they couldn't fully light up the place. It was a little scary as the temperature was also very high in that area.

The kids were home schooled for a while, as the schools were not adequate enough. They couldn't understand why were they here? Why Lakshmi was not attending school like before? But she forgot all of it fleetingly and adjusted to the new environment along with her siblings and family.

As Lakshmi's father became busy with work, all the life that they were used to was left behind in the city. The days became more hectic. There were days when the kids didn't see their father at all, as he became busy with establishing the project. The work was progressing very fast and a lot of new families were arriving and joining the company. Recruiting people to the assigned posts was also a task along with other duties .

As Lakshmi's father had to travel a lot for work, her mother was in charge of the house, taking care of all the kids and the grandparents. One of Lakshmi's favorite times of the day was to spend time with her grandmother, who would tell them stories about Gods and their powers. She insisted on worshipping the Gods daily in the morning and would spend most of her time praying, spreading and incorporating culture along with spirituality in the house.

Around this time Lakshmi started learning cycling. Her father believed that before the fear kicks in, a child should learn to override it. His philosophy was before completion of age 5, one should be done with cycling lessons. While in class 6-7 through with scooter/bike riding and by class twelve should be able to drive a car.

Coming back to Lakshmi's routine. She was learning cycling, home schooling and adjusting to all these big changes in her life. Her plate was full with trying to tackle these situations while meeting new people and making new friends.

First commission of the project was over and the management had taken the steps to construct a planned, large scale gated community for the employees with schools, hospitals, shopping center, movie area, clubs, parks, and sport centers. One important aspect of this colony construction was to plant a lot of plants.

Planting a lot of trees and plants to tackle the heat in the area worked out very impressively. After a couple of years as the trees grew big, the temperatures in the area dropped by a few degrees.

Chapter 2

Animal Experience

The project was getting accomplished faster than imagined and was also getting shaped up well. The employees and their families were being taken care of. The management had planned a very well organized, temporary township with plans of building a permanent township with more amenities. Temporary town ship consisted of just the quarters, a common park and a shopping complex. Rest of the amenities, like entertainment, health care etc. were taken care of by the village nearby as the nearest city was at five hours drive.

Lakshmi resumed her schooling in a nearby community which was also a company owned township established much earlier and possessed all amenities. They had a school where kids from her community went to study, until Lakshmi's community could have its own.

One funny incident happened while attending school. Suddenly, loud bells rang followed up by an announcement asking to shut down all the windows and doors of the classes, and to stay inside till further announcement. Everyone in the class started to panic as it was the last class for the day, after which everybody was supposed to leave for their homes. Even the teacher didn't have much information regarding it as she was also informed along with the students itself. The kids felt nervous as it felt like school arrest. Kids started to discuss among themselves the possibilities due to which a lot of noise was produced in the room. Teacher silenced the class, instructing that no one should leave, warning the kids not to come out of the classroom and stand in the corridor.

Lakshmi was appointed the class monitor and her teacher assigned her to oversee the class. Teacher left the classroom to find out about the situation. Up until she came back, Lakshmi had to see to it that none of the student got up from their desks and made any noise. As she stood at her teacher's desk, monitoring the class, a loud siren was heard by everyone going around in the colony. The class started to whisper loudly and frightened, thus making a lot of noise. Lakshmi tried silencing them but nobody listened to her, ultimately, she shouted loudly to silence the room and then suddenly the class door opened and their teacher along with another teacher entered the class. Looking at her, Lakshmi was terrified but the teacher calmed her down and asked her to take her seat while locking the door. Silencing the class, she announced that she had information to share about the situation and she could do so only when the class was silent. Suddenly the class became silent with all eyes following and resting on the teacher.

She began by reassuring that there's nothing to worry about. The issue was that a wild bear had entered the colony. He had went inside a house, ransacked it and harmed the inmates before running off. Neighbors saw the incident and immediately informed the police. Then the whole police force started searching out for the bear and thus it was announced that it was quite dangerous to venture out. The instructions to stay indoors were given by the police asking everybody to stay put until further notice. All the students were in a confused state!! They were still confused as they should be happy about the situation or frightened. Whole class was afraid to death, sitting in pin drop silence including the teachers who were sitting beside each other but not talking, which had never happened before. The silence continued for 30-45 minutes, after which they all heard another announcement asking only the teachers to gather at the principal's office.

Again, the class was left under Lakshmi's supervision and unlike before, silence prevailed in the room. She didn't have much to do as all the frightened faces were looking at her. She stood confidently, not expressing her feelings as beneath the confidence she was shit scared too. Within 15 minutes, the teacher was back and this time with a big beaming smile. She shared with the class that the wild bear was caught by the police which was then brought to the colonies police station. Furthermore, the inspector along with the principal had arranged for all the students to visit the station and have a view of the bear. For that all the classes had to form lines in the playground and leave for the station from there. Students got super excited to be able to see the bear up close . Lakshmi being the class monitor was leading the class behind the teacher. It was for the first time that Lakshmi would be seeing a police station and a bear, she thought while forming the line. Reaching the station, she saw the constables with rifles in uniforms, which was a scary sight to start with.

Nearing them they looked quite friendly, happy with the days job which changed the vibe of the place. From one side of the gate the student's line was entering the police station while from other side the line was coming out with a lot of hustle and bustle. . The entering lines were silent, not knowing what to expect. Lakshmi took the line into the gates encountering more police personals looking proud of their achievement. Moving inside Lakshmi saw a big wild bear. The bear was kept in a cage. It was a pitiful sight to watch the bear in that state. Unknowingly the bear had come into colony (Human habitat). Might be out of its own fear had attacked people for which he had to be in this situation. Lakshmi was deep in her thoughts when she vaguely heard her name being called from behind. She turned back and saw a police inspector calling her. She couldn't recollect the person. He came, held her hand and took her into the cabin. Lakshmi again turned back this, time looking at her teacher and classmates staring back making the whole situation very tense.

Inside the cabin she focused on the inspector, and on closer inspection she realized that he was one of her father's friends who visited them frequently along with his family. It's just that she had never seen him in his uniform before and neither did she know he worked as an inspector. Everybody was looking at them which made the whole situation a little tense. He made her sit, asking about her father and offered a cool drink in between. Lakshmi felt privileged at the treatment in front of her class friends. As soon as Lakshmi finished her drink, her uncle immediately got up from his chair and held her hand guiding her towards another door. He took her near the bear asking her to pick some fallen hair for remembrance, which she did in front of all. He packed it in a cover and gave it to her. She asked her uncle what they would do with the bear. Laughing out loud he informed her they would leave the bear in the forest again. After that she again joined the line leaving the police station. All the kids surrounded her asking her a lot of questions. The teacher hushed everybody. Reaching school, everybody picked their bags and left for their respective homes. After going home, Lakshmi narrated the whole incident to parents, grandparents and siblings, and showed them her prized possession of bear's hair. Then Lakshmi freshened up, finished homework, ate and went to bed dreaming about the next day.

Next day in school, during the prayer the principal explained the whole incident in detail and appreciated all the students for maintaining the decorum. By afternoon, after the school, Lakshmi's community kids were waiting for the bus to pick them up. When the kids saw the bus coming, they started running towards the it, but as they were standing too near to the bus somebody pushed her from behind.... and in that moment, one tire of the bus went above Lakshmi's feet. Before she could even realize one of the seniors, was already carrying her, running towards the hospital. After proper supervision of the legs, the doctor confirmed that all was fine. The bus driver had brought the bus directly to the hospital where he picked them all and dropped at the township. She experienced little pain, as she walked home slowly to thinking that the excitement still continued from the previous day and wondered what was in store for her tomorrow?

With passing days, in no time the new township was ready to be occupied. The township had a shopping center, community halls, stadiums, swimming pools, hospital, separate clubs for officers/staff and also an open movie theatre. It was such an interesting concept. The open theatre was well planned with grass growing at one end while a big white wall was constructed on the other on which the movies were displayed through a projector. Sundays in clubs, the movie to be played was displayed on the board. Either you could sit on the grass or else carry your own chairs. Lakshmi's grandmother would never miss any of the movies, making the staff carry chairs and the kids would tag along with her. The best part, also the true beauty of watching movies in open theatre was, when it rained. Couple of times the movie was stopped abruptly in the middle. Then the viewers got smarter and started carrying umbrellas along with them. They not only carried one for themselves but even separate ones for the projector and the person who operated it. Lakshmi's grandmother would sit next to him, making sure he played the entire movie whereas kids would play in rain while watching the movie. One day while screening, a rain song started playing in the movie while it was actually raining too and everybody started dancing in the rain. Later, the whole family went home soaking wet. Lakshmi's parents were having dinner by the time they reached home. They saw them coming all drenched and Lakshmi's father burst out laughing. Without any hesitation they dragged their parents into the rain making it even, and then everybody was soaked to the bone. It was such a beautiful night that Lakshmi would never forget in her lifetime.

In the new bungalow allotted to her father in the township, for the first time Lakshmi got her own room. Till then, one bedroom was shared among all the siblings. Lakshmi was overwhelmed seeing her room and to be able to have her own personal space. She decorated the room, assembled the furniture and made the room look beautiful and comfortable. It was kind of a luxury for her. Whoever came visiting to the house, she would drag them to her room, showing off her space and talked about posters on the walls without taking a no for an answer!!!

All the employees felt the need for a temple in the township. A committee was setup for designing and construction for the same. Foremost issue was the question about which idol of the God was to be placed in the temple. After a lot of discussions and meetings, they decided to construct Lord Swamy Aiyappa's Temple (Elder son of Lord Shiva). Lakshmi had heard the name of the God for first time as before that she had never heard about this God. Her source of God's information was her grandmother who hadn't enlightened her about this particular God. When Lakshmi asked her about Swamy Aiyappa, she shared stories about the lord. Huge discussions were happening in the colony as to how the idol looks like and the specialty of Swami Aiyappa. Few months later as the temple started taking shape, all the doubts vanished as it was shaping up quite well. Temple was ready in no time for people to worship. Lakshmi's family along with her maternal aunt's family went for darshan to the temple. That day she was dressed in a black dress; the God's idol was also made of black colour. To which her aunt commented that she was matching with God's idol. She didn't understand the context so didn't respond. . All of them sat in the temple and ate the prasad served, and later left for home on feet since it was near. .

As the next day was a Sunday, Lakshmi got up a little late and joined the elders who were having their early morning coffee. Temple with echoed with enthusiasm as it rang with Swamy Aiyappa's songs, which was audible inside the house from the distance. Incidentally, she was again wearing black to which her aunt started teasing her again saying that the songs were being played as she was again matching with the idol. From then onwards, she started calling her Aiyappa in a teasing manner. Even after many years she still called her Aiyappa reminding her of those days. Younger days were different falling for the fun of it as she grew being called by God's name she was conscious.

The temple was situated on a little hill. After finishing her homework Lakshmi would daily ride her cycle to the hill and roll back very fast, it was a game to her. . Around that time, evening poojas were being performed in the temple. One such day when she was taking her cycle out, Lakshmi's maternal uncle said that he was leaving as he had come to visit them for the weekend, to which Lakshmi waved bye and left cycling. When she came back from cycling her uncle was still at home. Lakshmi asked him why didn't he leave? He said because she didn't hadn't said goodbye properly even though he had spent an entire weekend with them. He taught her to care for people consistently and not to shower affection seasonally.

It was a normal day in Lakshmi's life, going to school attending all classes, coming back home, finishing her homework and then getting ready for the next day. One day, Lakshmi's mother called her, asking her to fetch some tomatoes from her friend's place. She obediently listened to her stepped out of the house. Realizing that it was getting dark, she decided to make a run for their house and return fast. She started running and reached their home in no time. Aunty asked her to rest a little and sit down, have some water while she brought the tomatoes. Lakshmi sat down and started chatting with her friend (aunt's daughter) forgetting the time. A while later she suddenly realized that it might be too late and even darker by now. Grabbing tomatoes, Lakshmi immediately left for her home, once again running back to beat the darkness. While doing so, she saw a few street dogs running after her. Lakshmi ran faster with dread watching more dogs joining the pack. By now five dogs were chasing her. She bravely tried to shoo them away by throwing stones at them, for which she had to stop running. Instead of going away, the dogs fearlessly formed a circle around her and simultaneously started inching closer, towards her. Lakshmi looked around for help and in the pitch-darkness could see nobody around. By now Lakshmi had given up all hopes, as fear struck, she looked helplessly towards the furious dogs. Lakshmi started screaming and jumping as the dogs progressed towards her. Suddenly, from nowhere a watchman came racing with a stick in his hand. He started hitting the dogs with the stick, moving Lakshmi away from them. In no time, all the dogs fled away from the spot and by then, Lakshmi felt relieved. The watchman accompanied her, dropping her home and advised her to always have somebody along, more so when going out in the evenings or nights. He told her not to be scared any more as the situation was sorted out. Lakshmi thanked him many times as for her he had appeared as a God in the pitch darkness to save her. She knew the alternate horrible scenario, where the night would have ended totally differently.

Chapter 3

Road Travel

All the kids had grown up by now and entered middle school. During one of the summer vacations Laxmi's father planned a road trip for all of them. That year he bought a new fiat car, which he wanted to test by taking the long drive. At home, preparations for the trip began. All were advised to travel light as the luggage had to fit in the trunk. Some snacks along with other food items and soft drinks also took some space in the dicky. Extra tire, a long thick rope, some mechanical things were also in the back. As luggage was huge, a carrie was fixed on the top of the car where some of the luggage was tied with the rope. . There was cassette player in the car so, Lakshmi packed her own music cassettes to listen to while travelling.

The trip was to visit Madras, Mahabalipuram & Pondicherry. As there was no digital help in those days, they bought a lot of road maps along with direction guides. Grandparents along with staff were left at home as they couldn't take such a long road travel. Now who sits where was the big question. After a lot of permutation and combinations, kids chose their places and settled in, waiting for their father to start , but then he entirely changed the setting arrangement. Luckily Lakshmi got to sit in front in, between her mother and father. She could also put her legs around the gear box. Rest of the kids were instructed to sit in the back. The journey started and it took two days to cross the state border and enter into another state. They took a couple of breaks during nights and covered most of the distance during daytime.

They reached Madras in the morning during breakfast time. Instead of checking into the hotel, Lakshmi's father directly took them to a nice breakfast point. They ordered their famous idli, dosa, vada and coffee. By the time everybody freshened up coming back to the car, they saw that the staff was ready with breakfast near the car itself. Seeing around, they observed that there was no sitting space and wondered how they will serve? They asked them all to sit in the car than attached trays to all the four doors serving breakfast in a novel way. They had never ate food in the car like this before. Lakshmi enjoyed the experience of eating inside the car along with her family while listening to music.

Later they checked into a hotel with a beautiful swimming pool. That was the first thing all the kids noticed. Hurriedly they shifted the luggage into rooms and in no time, they were at the pool. All of them were there except Lakshmi's father Mr. Venkat who announced that he'll join them a little later, after a small power nap. It was mid-afternoon by the time they finished the pool activity. Everybody was hungry and ready for lunch. After finishing with lunch they took a small nap and then got ready to explore the city. In their three days stay, they had covered important places in the city and did a lot of shopping. Next day, early morning they planned to leave for Mahabalipuram.

During the journey Lakshmi was assigned the job of DJ to play music, which others desired, by changing the cassettes regularly. There were many fights involved at times, which even led to halting the music altogether. Together they played a few games, ate snacks, making the rounds in the car. The journey totally turned out to be huge hit fun time.

Mahabalipuram is a historic place with some part of it immersed in the sea. They took a lot of pictures enjoying the place with its beautiful architectural work. Kids felt lucky to be exposed to all that so early in life. In between there was one big crocodile's zoo. All the kids were super excited to see the animal in reality. Observing the ruins of Mahabalipuram adjacent to sea was entirely different from the city lifestyle of Madras where they had spent the previous few days (so varied style of living in such small radius). Again, she thought that the city lifestyle was nothing to the way they were living in the colony. They stayed overnight in the Mahabalipuram town as it got dark. They planned to leave for Pondicherry early in the morning. As they headed to the town during the small journey Lakshmi fell asleep in the car, tired due to the journey.

They started early in the morning and reached Pondicherry earlier than expected. Entering the town, it looked very different from the usual Indian towns. Lakshmi's father explained that it's a Union Territory, also largely influenced by the Portuguese culture. Lot of Portuguese had settled in that place from long ago which reflected the influence in the town and all its aspects. They parked the car, got down and walked near the shore of the beach. Visited the famous Asharam. It was so peaceful everywhere. They could feel the mix of culture in the place, which had a huge impact on Lakshmi. By evening they had checked into a nice room attached to the Ashram in its enclosed premises. After freshening up and having an early dinner they called in the day early. In the room, the kids had just started playing when suddenly the lights went off. Their mother and father who were in the adjacent room came to the kids' room with a torch. In the dark night with no noise pollution, they could clearly hear the sound of the sea waves. Mr. Venkat asked them to listen to the rhythm of the waves and how beautiful it all sounded. Hearing the sounds, all of them went to the window to look at the sea. In the moonlight the waves and sea were projecting such a marvelous view that it can't be expressed in words. Slowly waves became big, each wave coming close to the compound wall of the Ashram. Unexpectedly the waves started hitting the walls with water spelling over the wall. Mr. Venkat explained that the sea behaves different to moon creating bigger waves wherein it resides back with smaller waves during daytime under sun's influence on water. He asked them to observe the sea in the morning. Suddenly lights lit up, electricity was back. It was getting late so everybody decided to sleep. In the morning, all of them got up and the first thing Lakshmi did was to look at the sea. It had gone back unlike the last night, exactly as Mr. Venkat had told them. That day they played by the beach for a long time as the water was irresistible. Around evening they explored the city.

It was time to start the journey back home. This time while travelling Lakshmi along with her elder brother sat in the front. Lakshmi's mother sat at the back with the other kids.. After two days of travel Lakshmi's elder brother felt like driving the car for a while. Lakshmi's father was a little hesitant as he was not an experienced driver, and it was a highway they were travelling on. Still, he kept on insisting so Mr. Venkat had to oblige letting him drive. He was driving fine while Mr. Venkat sat next to him until they a hit traffic jam on highway, which was a two-lane road. They had to stop the car for a long time getting impatient as Lakshmi's brother overtook the car in front. As he entered the next lane big speeding bus headed towards them from the front. The driver responded immediately and pulled the bus down the road creating space for the car. A major accident was avoided or else the consequences would have been devastating. They took the car off the road slowly Lakshmi's brother was still behind the steering wheel. As he stopped the car and got down from car, he shivered, thoroughly shaken. Laxmi's father calmed him down without scolding or shouting and handled the situation well by comforting the boy reassuring that all was well. He made him drink some water and sat behind the steering wheel himself. Mr. Venkat again started the journey back home. By then, the traffic had also settled and the road had cleared up. Traffic jam took a toll on Mr. Venkat's plan as they couldn't reach the desired destination on time. The day was coming to an end and it was getting dark. Inside the car everybody was silent and the outside darkness added up to the situation. After covering certain distance, the car made a big sound and stopped working. After trying to start the ignition a couple of times, the car did not respond. Mr. Venkat asked none of them to get down from the car expect for Lakshmi's elder brother. Both went in front of the car, discussed, came back and informed something had broken down which they have to get repaired . No other way but to stop vehicles passing by for help. Few cars went by but none of them stopped and also it was getting darker as time passed by. It was a scary situation and all of them were super tensed. Unexpectedly one truck driver stopped and enquired about the situation.

Accessing the situation the truck driver suggested, that the car needs to be taken to a garage and can't be fixed otherwise. As he was a frequent traveler on that way, he told Mr. Venkat that the town was nearby. Around the outskirts of the town, they could find many garages to get the car repaired. Now the issue was how could they take the car with so many people to the mechanic's garage? Even if they could get somebody (mechanic) he couldn't fix the car without adequate equipment. Truck driver came up with a solution to tie the car to the truck and pulling it along with the family. Laxmi's father asked if that would be possible to which he replied that he had done it before so it was doable. The long rope came into use. Both the ropes ends were tied to car at one end truck to the other end. Truck pulled the entire car slowly to the garage. Driver had charged for the service. A big relief was seen on Mr. Venkat's face, he said that even though he's charging they were very lucky that they got such a facility at that time. The truck driver pulled the car into a garage and made sure those people could do the job before he dropped them and left. The family thanked him for the timely helped and paid the amount he asked for. The garage owner promised to get the car repaired by next morning. He dropped the family in a hotel in his car in the city. Only to be back in the morning with their car which he promised would be delivering at the hotel itself.

Next day as soon as the car was handed over, the travel began. This time without any adventures, the family reached their home safely. Kids resumed school as vacations came to an end. Laxmi was eager to go to school as she had so much to share with her friends. Also to find out how her friends had spent their vacation.

Different kinds of organizations were formed in the colony one of them being the ladies club. Ladies of the colony were members who had to contest election among themselves to elect a management team. Ladies took up lot of social service activities in the nearby villages. Committee members planned many recreational activities. Laxmi's mother was elected to head the organization. Laxmi was very fond of music, dance and showed keen interest in the events. She participated in plays, fancy dress completions, group dances and more. Every year, the ladies club held annual day event in a big way. Laxmi always got the opportunity to participate in such events. Laxmi thought that the emphasis was focused mainly on stage but the fun part was at the backstage where in the assigned space everyone got ready. In so much chaos and confusion, still everybody got ready with costumes, makeup at the right time. The event happened in the indoor auditorium of the colony. For the annual day's celebration generally most of the seniors got picked up. Laxmi thought she was fortunate enough to get such a chance in the colony events at least.

Another such organization formed was Bengali's organization. As the company was growing, number of people moving into the colony was increasing. Henceforth, this organization too had good number of volunteers. For the organizations presence to be felt they planned to celebrate Durga pooja in Bengali style.

They zeroed on a place picking up a garden near to Laxmi's house. Preparations started for the pooja. A temporary shed was buildup. One day while going the to school Laxmi noticed that a few trunks were present near the garden unloading a bunch of things. It struck to Laxmi that kids won't be able to play in the play area of the garden until the Pooja finishes, wondering how long it will take? Coming back from school she saw more people on the ground. Reaching home Laxmi's mother told her that some artisans had come down from Calcutta to make the idol of Goddess. Laxmi got excited to be able to see the making of Kali ma. It would take more than a few months to build such a big idol. It had become a routine for Laxmi and her friends to visit the construction site while going and coming from school. They would spend time watching and understanding the process of making the idol. Due to regular visits, they got a little friendly with the artisans. They spoke only Bengali and no other language. Day by day the idol was taking a beautiful shape of Ma Durga sitting on a lion, killing the demon with a sword, conquering over the evil. The Goddess was dressed up with Bengali saree and jwellery reflecting their culture. Once the idol was finished making, work for construction of pandal started. Where the idol would be placed for worship. They created a mini-Calcutta type Durga pooja ambience in the garden. The organization people had really worked hard to make it happen.

Everybody was so happy by the outcome. Pooja was celebrated for ten days. As per their culture, food was served at the pandal. Even the cooks were brought from Calcutta to have that authentic touch. Khichadi, Tomato Chutney was compulsory to which other vegetarian dishes were added along with mishti doi. According to their customs, they had to wear new clothes every day for all ten days wherein they planned their year-long shopping needs. Every evening, some cultural activities were held for entertainment like games, orchestra, flower decoration, rangoli competition likewise. As the celebrations came to an end, Laxmi realized how fast time had passed by. Everybody went back to their normal lives. In school, exams had started which kept the kids along with parents very busy.

The plant was being constructed at a very fast pace. During this time, a team of engineers had come from Italy for some construction and erection work in the plant. They were given accommodations in the colony. Around summer time, their families also visited them. It was for the first time that Laxmi got exposed to the foreign people and their culture. The women wearing bikinis would sunbath as sunlight was something they crave for. Though in the colony it was a scandalizing topic. At the same time kids had a merry time, as their children would play hide and seek with them. During play time they would share chocolates with them, which tasted very different.

This vacation Laxmi's father planned to visit their hometown, Vishakhapatnam, where he was constructing their own, new house. It was semi ready, making certain portions apt for staying. The word of their relocation spread around, causing a lot of family members to visit them including many aunts, uncles and cousins. One of the cousins had a bike, he was elder among them and went to the college. He used to visit them on his bike. Looking at him ride, even Laxmi wanted to ride. Somehow, she convinced her cousin to provide her teaching classes on riding the bike. After the conversation, he assured her that she could pick it up very fast as she could already ride a cycle and hence understood balancing well. Laxmi's cousin was convinced that now it was her father who needed to give her permission first. Laxmi along with her cousin found Mr. Venkat sitting on terrace explaining work to a supervisor. Nervously, she approached him and expressed her desires to which her cousin joined, assuring that he will take utmost care while teaching her. To Laxmi's surprise Mr. Venkat gave permission on one condition, instructing she had to learn scooter first. Laxmi's cousin let Mr. Venkat knew that he only had a bike. The supervisor standing next to Laxmi announced that he had a scooter, and could spare for her to learn. It was a manual scooter with gears. Laxmi took some time first to be able to balance the scooter. As she got hold of it getting confident in balancing then she started to learn to manually change the gears. Initially the synchronization took time, getting the scooter jump in first gear. Within a week she was riding the scooter well . Laxmi even took her father on a scooter ride. He got convinced and permitted her to learn the bike eventually. Laxmi's cousin shifted her on the bike, wherein the gears were similarly manual while the only difference being that they were placed at the foot. Laxmi was a fast leaner and her brother became confident in her driving skills, and decided to shift to main road with traffic gradually. The road was adjacent to the beach, it was fun experience - the bike learning lessons. The beach offered a beautiful view with cold breeze around as she rolled past swiftly on the bike. She felt as if she was floating .

Chapter 4

Bus Ride

In the middle of night, Laxmi's mother woke up all the kids, as their father was back from the official tour of Europe. Everybody waited anxiously, as the door opened and he walked in through it. Kids went running, hugging him tightly. After having a round of tea Laxmi's father started sharing his experiences. Everyone was so immersed in the talk that they all completely forgot about the time. Suddenly Mr. Venkat remembered that he had brought a lot of gifts and asked the kids to open suitcases, which were also brand new. Mr. Venkat was a frequent traveler and he would always get interesting stuff for them hence, the kids couldn't wait for the suitcases to open. He didn't disappoint with this trip either. Kids started opening all the suitcases one after another and out came clothes, Chocolates, Souvenirs, electronic gadgets among which the camera was latest, wireless headphones, cassette player, remote control car and many fancy things. In this scenario, nobody was ready to go to school the next day. Laxmi's father declared holiday for all. Morning turned out to be an even bigger celebration as people kept on coming to meet Mr. Venkat. But kids were busy in their own world playing with all new stuff in the house. Mr. Venkat had taken plenty of pictures with the camera, which he brought in rolls. Gave the rolls to company photographer to develop them into pictures.

His official trip happened to be huge success as he had taken with a delegation. Laxmi's father was at the peak of his career, the fruits of which the entire family was enjoying.

That morning breakfast was a remarkable one where the whole family sat together after a long gap. The kids were waiting for their father to join them eagerly. Entering the room, he waved at everybody and went straight into the garden leaving everyone wondering why he didn't join them and instead went to the garden. Soon later, the backdoor opened and he walked in, this time with a ripened papaya in his hands. He always advocated kids to have fruits and salads along with meals. Laxmi had a great influence of her father while growing up. He was her superhero, who could just do anything. Laxmi's mother also played an impressive role model putting her in touch with culture and customs and developing healthy relationship with all family members.

After the exhausting trip Mr. Venkat desired a break, and planned a weekend trip to Hyderabad. In the city Laxmi's, maternal aunt and uncle were living whom they planned to visit while in town. The travel time to the city was five hours, so they always took the (midway break) at one of Mr. Venkat's friends places and then resuming the rest of the journey. By the time they reached Hyderabad it was quite late and they directly checked into a hotel. Kids had to share room among themselves. They were given a suite room, which was huge along with a lavish bathroom containing a bathtub. Before entering the city, they crossed the fruits market of custard apple, which appeared up only during the season. They stopped by and Mr. Venkat bought an entire basket of custard apple. Since they were rare and only available during this season, everybody in the family relished the fruit very much and Laxmi's father even planned to save the fruits for that night's dinner. After freshening up, they went to their parent's room where on the floor papers were spread, putting the big basket of fruits in the middle. That being the dinner arrangement for the night, Laxmi thought it was going to be an interesting dinner. They started eating enjoying the fruits. While eating Laxmi's father showed her two fruits asking her to pick one. She observed one fruit keenly which was ripe nicely but smaller than the other whereas the other one was big but not that ripened. Immediately she picked the big one to which her father laughed and asked her why did she choose that particular one? Innocently, she answered as she could eat more of the fruit. He made her eat both the fruits asking which was tastier? Smaller fruit was much tastier than the bigger one. Then Mr. Venkat advised her always to choose quality over quantity, as it would always be a better choice. Laxmi never forgot and applied that lesson in all spheres of life. Following day, the kids wanted to have a bath in the bathtub. Laxmi wanted to get into the bathtub right from the time she saw it first. She filled the tub with foam into which all the kids hopped in together. They enjoyed bath for long time until their mother dragged them out asking them to get dressed fast.

Laxmi's maternal aunt was married with kids whereas her uncle was still a bachelor. Laxmi's father was a very practical man, and he wanted his kids to be exposed to all kinds of lifestyles. When Laxmi's young uncle came to visit them, Mr. Venkat asked him to take all the kids to watch a movie in the theatre. He asked them to take them by bus not an auto but only by bus. They all dressed up and went to the bus station from where they took the bus for theatre. Standing at the bus station, she understood the networking of the buses which was done by number system. It was an interesting concept to learn. The other rule being women were supposed to enter the bus through the front door whereas men had to get in through the rear door. They also had to split in two groups. Laxmi's uncle instructed the girls to get down after two stops not before that. Bus was full, so girls got to stand next to the driver with clear view of the road. Laxmi thought it would be easy to count stops for them to get down. Bus started from the stop and gradually driver increased the speed. From nowhere Laxmi saw a bull appearing on the road running along with the bus. It raced towards a scooter who was coming in the opposite direction. He was on an average speed but as the bull ragged on him he changed lanes and crashed on to the bus going under it. There was such a hue and cry in the bus, some started shouting, few crying and a lady whispering that she's too scared to see blood all over the place. Laxmi also started imagining the man dead, crushed under the tire. Suddenly the conductor appeared from the back of the bus asking everybody to get down. With a lot of fear, the sisters got down looking straight and joining the rest of the family. All the passengers were standing on the pavement not knowing what to do amidst which the driver of the bus fled the scene. People were too scared to peep down expecting some police help to come and handle the situation. In the whole confusion among the hustle bustle Laxmi saw a small man coming from under the bus dragging the scooter along. Everybody kept looking at the guy expecting the unexpected. One person among the crowd helped pulling him out along with his scooter. By God's grace though he went under the bus luckily, he fell between the two tires along with the scooter, which made such a big sound. As they pulled him from under the bus and checked him thoroughly. Putting the scooter aside they made the person sit offering him some water.

Fortunately, except for few scratches he didn't have any major injuries . Pulling the scooter, they made it stand on its stand, trying to kick start it. On the very first kick it rolled up immediately. Laxmi thought definitely that it was his lucky day. Police came and they took charge of the situation. Arranged another bus for passengers. Unfortunately, the kids disobeyed their father and took an auto to reach theatre as they were falling short of time. Luckily, they could make it on time without missing any part of the movie. More than the movie, Laxmi was eager to share the incident with her father. Eventually after the

movie they went back to hotel and narrated everything animatedly. Mr. Venkat heard the story with lot of tension finally when they finished, he laughed it over.

Chapter 5
Spirituality

Laxmi's grandmother was a big devotee of God. Daily pooja at their home was performed by her. She made sure that all the rituals and festivals were followed properly. Because of her the household had its share of spiritual connection going on. Spiritual calendar throughout the year was followed dedicated to various Gods.

One such month was Karthik Purnima , wherein Lord Shiva was worshipped.. In this month, basic ritual was getting up before sunrise, taking a head bath, fasting and then performing pooja of lord Shiva, before starting the day. Follow the same rituals in night break the fast with dinner after winding up the day. You needed to follow vegetarian diet throughout whole month. It's considered to be fortunate if you are able to take a dip in Ganges in this auspicious month. Very close to the colony, river Godavari passed by. Buses were arranged from the colony people to avail the facility if willing to take the dip in the river. Mostly the bus was filled with women and kids. Laxmi's grandmother too planned to take the bus. Mr. Venkat asked the kids to accompany her. It was dark outside as everyone started to get into the buses and soon buses were filled with devotees. Devotional songs were being played which created a pious atmosphere. Reaching the river bed, Laxmi observed that the sun was just rising spreading orange color though out the sky, also the sun rays were dancing on the water creating a mesmerizing view. Though Laxmi was sleepy looking at the view, hurriedly she got down from the bus and exited. .

Everybody had made their personal tents with towels and sarees to change before getting into the water. The water was extremely cold but that didn't stop the devotees, utilizing their chance to please the Gods they dove in. After three dips elders performed the pooja for the sun God. Later on, the devotees lighted diyas leaving them in the river. Kids were still playing in the water. The buses were ready to leave, everybody finished their pooja and changed into dry clothes and headed back to the colony. Laxmi ran into the house as it was getting late for school. She had to again, catch the school bus hence, she dressed up fast and finished breakfast, took the packed tiffin box and left the house.

Laxmi's father decided to visit Saibaba Puttaparthi with family. Sai Baba proclaimed himself to be reincarnation of Shirdi Sai baba. He had a lot of devotees from different countries, who believed in him and his powers. He would produce Vibhuti from nowhere handing it over to devotees. Entering the town Laxmi saw that he had transformed the whole place. He constructed a very big Ashram for himself. Different complexes were built for devotees, schools, college, hospital multiple purposes. It looked like lot of funds were being generated. Sai Baba would give darshan once in the morning, followed up in the evening again. In the Morning when the family went for the darshan sometime later the self- proclaimed god man came in a wheelchair waving at the crowd. It was not impressive enough to believe his words. Mr. Venkat said he felt like some unfinished work, proceedings the trip further by visiting Lord Venkateshwara at Tirupati. The family left for Tirupati directly from there. Though they had visited Tirupati before many times, kids were all quite young at that time . Laxmi had grown now and was able to understand a lot of the surroundings. To reach Tirumala they had to cross the Ghat section which was a new experience for Laxmi. It looked a little scary at the beginning but as she got the hang of it, she started enjoying the journey. Entering the main gate, they saw that the whole area was covered with beautiful flowers of different varieties. Going ahead you could see the whole town decorated with flowers. Laxmi had never seen anything like that. The flowers arrangement looked rare, making the temple look extraordinary like the God's work. Expecting nothing like that, Laxmi's father enquired about the celebrations. They came to know the festivity was called 'Brahma Utsavam' and it lasted one whole month. Brahma Utsavam means a festival to commemorate an offering by Lord Brahma to Lord Vishnu. According to a legend, Lord Brahma performed a Brahma utsavam prayer for Lord Vishnu. That's why you will find Shiva, Brahma and Vishnu at the Suchidram Sthaumalaya temple, where offering are given daily. The town was richly decorated as God's idols were placed in ratham taking around the town performing rath yatra. Laxmi's family went to their rooms, had a proper bath and changed into traditional clothes joining the queue for God's darshanma. Laxmi's grandmother would always tell them stories about the almighty Gods. She would take them to temples for praying regularly but what was happening in front of them was altogether different as the magnitude with which everything was happening was unimaginable. It felt like God was present right there. Laxmi thought she was blessed to be able to watch such festivity. They could see the chariot coming towards them. From near the chariot, one could see the huge God's idols covered in heavy rare jewelry from head to toe. The whole festival had big influence on Laxmi, making her believe in God. The following day offered a proper Lord Venkateshwara darsham in temple after which, they started heading back home. They all wanted to stay back but the town was crowded with pilgrims . The rush was a hinder, being content with the darshnam they decided to leave. As years passed by, number of devotees visiting the festival increased three folds.

Laxmi always had thoughts that in spiritually it was proven Gods take care of everything and everybody wherein at school science was teaching some fundamentals and theories explaining reasons for existence. Now watching the festivity, she started having faith in Gods . The whole journey Laxmi kept asking questions to grandmother about her belief in God which she felt in the temple. Finding her interest Mr. Venkat bought Ramayana and Mahabharat for Laxmi to read and get more awareness about God.

Laxmi's household was full of food lovers. There were three generations residing together. Food had to cater to all, above that they always had some guest at home. From quite an early age Laxmi was used to helping her mother in the kitchen. First thing she learned was to make tea and coffee. One day when Laxmi was studying her mother called out for her. She immediately went downstairs to see her mother along with her friend's chit chatting. As she appeared Laxmi's mother with a proud smile asked Laxmi to prepare five cups of tea and three of coffee. All her friends were surprised wondering would she be able to manage all by herself? Laxmi went to kitchen thinking she had never prepared so many cups, but didn't want to disappoint her mother. The main part of making Laxmi did with some help from staff. After it was made, she arranged the cups in a tray along with biscuits and snacks serving to the guests. All the aunties were impressed helping themselves. Everybody praised Laxmi of her cooking skills that her mother is blessed to have a lovely grown-up girl around the house helping in kitchen.

In reality, Laxmi's elder brother was more interested in cooking. Once Laxmi's parents had to visit their hometown to attend their cousin's wedding. All the kids were responsible for cooking three meals at home, attending to the grandparents and making sure not to miss school either. In one of such occasions Laxmi learned cooking from her elder brother who was a wonderful cook. He taught her from basics, later went into detail which Laxmi grasped very fast.

It so happened when their cousins came visiting Laxmi's house in their break, that the foodie family planned an elaborate breakfast. Poori's with chicken curry was served as the kids started eating. One ate poori more than the other it got into serious competition. Poori' kept finishing in no time. Finally, one of the cousins won as he had eaten most of them. Discussing the winner with big appetite they realized how tired Laxmi's mother would be. To show her their gratitude they took up the job of preparing lunch for everybody. By now Laxmi had become a good cook she decided to prepare a dish all by herself. Rest of the kids too chose dishes, menu was set and the preparations started. The table was cleared, kitchen was cleaned and the music was on. It was so much fun cooking together with a slight competition as to whose dish would turn out to be the best. Laxmi thought group cooking was fun. Later as they ate together what they together had prepared turned out much more fun & they could not stop talking at top of their voices.

During festivals and Pooja's Laxmi's grandmother took charge of the kitchen, not allowing anybody inside as the food was prepared religiously for Gods.

She used to make very tasty traditional dishes on those special occasions only. Laxmi's grandmother would prepare with so much care and devotion in those days (food) everybody in the house use to look forward to it. On Diwali food used to be very elaborate and tasty. Kids couldn't choose between bursting crackers and eating.

Laxmi started to develop a very healthy relationship with cooking and food. To add up to that she took up some cooking classes of Chinese food as well as cake making classes. The teacher was a parsi lady who was taking classes in her free time. Laxmi observed that her style of cooking was entirely different from their house hold which was very interesting. Looking at her cook, it felt like cooking was so easy. The lady taught an evening snack which Laxmi thought she could easily prepare at home. Next day Laxmi bought ingredients and started preparing the dish. In the evening while the staff was preparing tea, she entered the kitchen and resumed making the dish where she had left off. Seeing Laxmi's prep, her father bought some friends along as he had so much confidence on his daughter, now that she was even attending classes. Midway of her cooking Laxmi realized that the snack was looking nothing like the one her teacher had made. Guests were waiting in the living room and she was left with no choice but to serve them. Looking at them eat what she had made Laxmi was feeling sorry for them. This was one of Laxmi's initial experience with cooking.

One unique experience for Lakshmi with cooking was when students of their class decided to go on a picnic. Girls were not much into it but then the boys convinced them. They told them that it would be fun as they planned to cook food in the picnic and eat together. Venue and date was fixed. They asked the girls to get nothing but only to join them for picnic. By the time, the girls gathered and went to the spot their fellow classmates were already there. They had placed bricks made two stoves out of them, preparing rice on one and chicken on another one. Don't know who & how but everything was very well planned. Laxmi told her friends she had never seen food being prepared this way before, to which they asked her does she even know how to cook? Even to boil eggs for a start, pulling her leg teasing her. It was a pleasant afternoon with all friends cooking together in a remote place and spending time together. While the food was being cooked, they played a few games. Meanwhile, the food was ready and everybody was famished by then . The pots were placed in the middle and all helped themselves with food. Eating food Laxmi could feel the difference in taste as food was prepared with charcoal and wood. Finished eating, they cleaned up the place and vessels.

They spent some time lying under the trees. Laxmi thought that Sunday was well spent with friends. Day was heading towards evening and everybody parted ways waving goodbyes to meet up at school next day.

During the festival season, Laxmi's mother always prepares some special food items. Lots of guests used to visit them around that time. One of school holiday she started by sorting out ingredients instructing the staff to put plate full of white flour in the balcony to dry under sun. The boy put the plate on the last step of the stairs opened the balcony door and left. Everybody got busy in their respective works and didn't notice. Suddenly winds started to blow in high speed while raining heavily. By now the flour had spread on rest of the steps rain water sprinkled on the stairs too. Hearing the rain sound Laxmi's mother called her brother to get the plate from balcony. Her brother responded went towards the stairs hurriedly not knowing the situation. The flour and water together made the steps so slippery that he slid down so fast and in a second, he was downstairs. Hearing the loud sound everybody came out. Before anybody could gauge the situation next two were skidding down the stairs one after another. Laxmi had her epic share of stair sliding moment. Though it was dangerous but it was still funny at the same time and everybody started laughing at each other. Luckily nobody was injured. Later they had to wash the stairs clean & dry it. In bed at night before sleeping, Laxmi was recollecting the day and laughing remembering everybody's expression. Shockingly the thought struck her that not only for cooking but the ingredients had multiple usages.

Chapter 6

Music

In Laxmi's house it was a daily ritual to play spiritual songs in the morning. Every morning after freshening up, everyone would gather in the living room with their respective beverages tea/coffee/milk and drink together while playing music in the background, read newspaper and have lots of discussion. Her father insisted the kids to read local, state and national newspapers. All kinds of papers were delivered in the morning especially a telugu one for their mother. Paper reading led to a lot of discussions on topics, if time permitted it would extend to the evening. Between which a rangoli was made in front of the door. The day used to start with such positivity that Laxmi would wait for early mornings. That's how important music was for Laxmi.

In middle school her mother had joined her in Kutchupudi and Sangeetham classes. Laxmi not understanding the cultural importance didn't give much time and quit quite early. Around the same time her father had bought a cassette player, which was more fun to hear and was convenient. For the player, her brother had bought a lot of cassettes not only of songs but movie stories too. In leisure all the kids would listen to the movie stories and pass time together. But then they would forward the songs to which Laxmi used to wait for but as majority wins they used to override her. Whenever she used to get alone time, she would listen to music in her own room. The music got her glued to the player, but slowly later on she started understanding the lyrics. She would note down the lyrics sing along and keep on learning that way. Her father had bought some top musical hits from Europe during his visit. When she listened to those cassettes, understood the vast difference in what she was listening. As she grew music became an integral part of her existence. Being exposed to music early she enjoyed all genres.

Her connection with music grew more as in school, and colony a lot of activities related to music took place. Then there was always the fun of singing songs on the school bus. That being one of Laxmi's favorite activities of the day. Antakshari was one of the games played by kids on the bus. In the colony, orchestras were arranged at regular intervals for entertainment.

One day after school when everybody was relaxing Laxmi's father came home asking everybody to get ready as he had some surprise in store for them. Hurriedly everybody dressed up fast and assembled near the car. Then he took them to the market place and stopped the car near a store asking everybody to get down. Laxmi couldn't see any clothes, jewelry or food store around while getting down, and kept wondering what the surprise was about? As they followed their father, they got into a very big music system store. Laxmi was amazed to see such a big store with huge music systems on display.

Till then she was using a cassette player, Walkman with headphone and similar stuff. She never had seen anything like this. A sales person came to address them, Laxmi's father spoke to him for a while and in the meantime Laxmi started scanning the whole store gazing at all the systems. The sales person started showing the latest models explaining its features in detail. After a lot of consultation and putting the price tag in view they zero downed on two systems. All thrilled Laxmi asked her father were they really going to buy now? Excitingly he asked Laxmi to pick any one among the two. They were repeatedly playing both the systems for them to get a hang of it. After her father asked her to pick one Laxmi started to listen more carefully. While hearing both the systems she heard difference in the output between the two systems. She shared her observation with rest of her family. Pointing out that one of the system's voice output was more clearer than the other system, so they should pick the one with good clear sound quality. They all observed, her father said good point and ultimately, they picked the one Laxmi had suggested. Just to walk into a store to pick a music system, taking along with them Laxmi had never even dreamed of anything like that! Now the issue was where it would be placed at home, with such big speakers. Laxmi's father already had a vision and said it will be stationed (mounted) on walls in the living room.

Next day Laxmi was super excited to go home early from school, as she wanted to hear music from the brand-new music system. By the time she reached home, installation was still going on. They were putting three stands on the wall for two speakers, one for the player. Until the work was finished, she decided to finish her homework joining back later. Work on mounting the system could not be completed that day and got extended to the following day as well. After it was all assembled then before switching it on, a small pooja was performed of the system also first God's song was played, than the chaos started on whose choice was to be next. Laxmi's father came up with a solution suggesting to play radio for a start and listen to music. Incidentally it was peak time for radio stations in the evening and such lovely numbers started playing everyone relaxed started enjoying the music and the system with small inbuilt lights which were dancing to the music. Later everybody adopted to the time schedule. Spiritual songs to start the day with followed by news than music. As kitchen was adjacent to the living room Laxmi would always play music while cooking.

Few of her cousin, Laxmi's father had given employment to also shifted to the colony. They were four of them who shared a bachelor pad her father had allotted for them. Once while cycling she went to their room just out of curiosity. They always got a lot of chocolates for kids and pampered them.

During her visit they were playing some music, which she never had heard before. As she listened, she liked it a lot. Checking with her cousins, they informed it was a kind of music called Gazals sung by a private artist. As she wanted to listen more, Laxmi borrowed the cassettes promising to return it later. They were more than happy to share it with her, which she bought home playing it on the new music system.

Instead of repeatedly being stopped by her family, she kept on singing along with the singers while playing the system. They complained about Laxmi spoiling all the fun of listening to music as she was not matching to the singing standard of the singer and nevertheless she continued. Once during an antakshari completion in the colony when their turn came her sister insisted Laxmi to sing as she was a very good singer. Laxmi thought its quite easy as she knew the song with the alphabet which she sang regularly. Confidently she took the microphone and started singing.

For the first time, she was listening to her own voice, and it was not what she was expecting of herself, she finished the song fast giving back the microphone even faster. After that for a while everyone was spared from Laxmi's voice.

Amongst all of this, life was going on smoothly. Suddenly Laxmi's father was transferred again, this time to a town though. By now the family had become comfortable in the colony surroundings, but they had to move to a new town again. Laxmi was very sad as she had to leave behind her school colony friends & teachers who were part of her daily life. . Coming from school Laxmi saw her father home, together her parents were packing along with the office staff. Kids were given two big boxes each where they had to pack all clothes in one the other one constrained to books, toys and miscellaneous. The boxes along with the car would come in a truck wherein the family would take a flight. It was for the first time Laxmi was travelling by plane, which kept her spirits high imagining what more would unfold for her in future. While the packing was going on in the house, Laxmi kept wondering how they would mount the car on to truck? She kept on asking her father about it, but better than explaining he asked her to accompany him. All of them went to a location where a ramp was built of the trucks height. The mover's driver drove the car from the ramp into the truck. It was quite interesting to watch the process after which a lot of discussion happened among kids. Finally, the day came when they had to leave the place. A big farewell was arranged on behalf of Laxmi's father as he was officially being sent on the next project. Few people spoke about Mr. Venkat's achievements, wishing him good wishes for his further endeavor.

The whole family shifted to the company's guest house with their daily needed luggage reliving the truck to go ahead with packages. They were prepared to catch the flight next day. Laxmi saw her father was excited to take them on their first flight. They had to change two planes to reach their destination. Though Laxmi wanted to explore the flight by herself her father didn't miss a chance explaining it all to them. Seeing her father's enthusiasm and over excitement Laxmi thought to sober down a little, sit back and enjoy the ride. When the plane landed Laxmi was a bit disappointed feeling like the journey ended too fast. Reaching the town, they checked into a hotel for a couple of days waiting for the truck. The company staff unloaded the truck, assembled the furniture, setup the kitchen leaving rest of the parcels for them to unpack. It almost took a week for them to settle down.

Settling down led to a hunt for schools. After thorough scrutiny, they zeroed down to a school in Airforce base. Laxmi's father took them to the school, on the way Laxmi saw them crossing a beautiful lake which led to a small hill top where the school was located. The admission process took a couple of hours after which the kids were informed to join classes from next day onwards. Returning back from school in the car Laxmi asked her father how they would go to school as there were no school buses?

Reaching home everybody got busy preparing for school packing books, setting the uniform so on. But the riddle of how to commute to school daily still remained unsolved. Knowing the situation, Laxmi's father had taken the house near to the school, he soon resolved the dilemma by suggesting cycles for everybody. Cycles were bought, making them all set for the new school. First day car escorted the kids while riding the cycles. Laxmi loved cycling so she enjoyed the ride, putting her backpack on the carrier she rode. As it was an exclusive air force base not much traffic was there on the road. The ride was smooth as the road was adjacent to the lake and the cool breeze flowing made the ride even merrier. Once the road took uphill it became tough to ride but later once, they got used to it, even that was enjoyable. As they entered the school, students showed them the parking slot taking them to their respective classes. From there, the teachers instructed them to leave their bags in classes and join the class line for assembly. On the first day Laxmi was very nervous as everything was new, nothing like her old school. As their class line moved towards the ground suddenly one of the teachers dragged Laxmi away from the line making her stand on the podium giving her a banquet in her hands to hold. Already she was nervous and on top of that she was put on stage facing the whole school on her first day. Another teacher came with more instructions, pointing towards an old teacher she informed Laxmi that today the Sanskrit teacher was retiring from her duty. That her felicitation will follow after the prayer finishes during which she will signal Laxmi to give the Sanskrit teacher the bouquet and later take her blessings and come back to where she was standing. During the assembly the principal, few teachers gave speeches about the Sanskrit teacher about the dedication with which she worked and guided students. Following which Laxmi presented the bouquet touched her feet and took her blessings. It looked all fine from far but as she approached the teacher, she saw tears in her eyes which she was controlling with difficulty, later she couldn't hold back and cried while giving her speech.

Returning back from assembly, school head boy asked her to meet the principal in his office before her joining classes. By the time Laxmi went to his office there was already a girl waiting outside the office door. Laxmi thought of going next after her and stood next to her waiting for her turn. The girl looked at Laxmi with a smile asking is she the same girl who gave flowers to the teachers today in assembly to which Laxmi nodded. She further asked that why was she punished for with a weird expression. Laxmi looked shocked to that and explained she was not there for punishment but principal had summoned her to meet him.

She laughed out loud, introducing herself as Poonam and shared that she was standing there for punishment. Further she told Laxmi that she was a regular, the school management informed her to wear the school skirt under the knee length which she differed to follow by wearing a miniskirt to school. Then Laxmi looked at the skirt, it was really of a very short length in anyway to be considered for school uniform. Poonam commented giving a quirky smile, they don't change rules I don't change the length of my skirt. Naughtily she continued my parents have given up on me now it's the principal's turn after which she will be free to be able to wear miniskirt to school. Laxmi was puzzled to come across such a person but still was getting impressed with her rebellious attitude. Talking to her they realized they were in the same class but in different sections. Poonam asked Laxmi to meet her in the recess where she'll introduce her to her friends. They parted ways and Laxmi went into the principal's office. As she entered principal welcomed her to the new school and informed that it was very courageous of her to take up the stage on first day, congratulating her and asked to join her class. Leaving the office Laxmi again met Poonam planning their meet again in recess. Laxmi looked at Poonam a little closely, she saw how beautiful she looked above that she was very friendly too. Laxmi entered the class taking permission from the class teacher who was taking attendance. Looking at her teacher said so you are the new admission? She introduced her to the class assigning the class monitor to update about the ongoing lessons and share notes and to take her seat. After few classes, the recess bell rang, Laxmi thought she could make friends with her fellow classmate later but had to meet Poonam first. Laxmi couldn't forget Poonam the whole while, as she was so impressed by her and wanted to make friends with her at any cost. Poonam's class was next to hers, and as Laxmi came out from her class, she heard her name being called , looking in that direction she saw Poonam surrounded by a few more girls waving at her. Laxmi met Poonam wherein she introduced Laxmi to her friends. They all lived in the colony, though they were from different sections but of same class. They were all from air force back ground Laxmi being the only outsider (civilian) in the group. As it was Laxmi's first day they showed her around the campus, which was quite big unlike her previous school. Lastly, they took Laxmi to the school canteen. Canteen man was very friendly with the girls, they looked regular at his place. Picked few chocolates along with samosa not missing the mirchi and chutney asking the canteen guy to pack the stuff. Laxmi thought they are packing food to eat in the class wondering which one as everybody belonged to different classes. Not knowing where they were going, she merely followed them. Hiding behind trees they slowly followed a narrow path which led to the lake's bank. As Laxmi looked around it was so beautiful with water all around, some clouds and the hilly area. They all sat while opening the snack packet everyone looked like they had no worries to which Laxmi asked them why are they looking so indifferent. Poonam replied with her mischievous smile that the area where they were sitting is a restricted zone and no kids can enter in that zonal area. Laxmi was horrified for having so many experiences on her very first day. Expecting not to be caught, she looked at Poonam thinking what more she could expect from this girl, at the same time she felt like a hero, breaking the rules.

Chapter 7

Bike Accident

They were seven girls altogether in the group. As time passed by, they became very close to each other. One of the things they all loved doing was to check display boards in the hallway. The whole school was divided into four groups and competitions were held among these groups. The seniors were selected to head the groups besides the head boy and girl. One of the tasks of these groups were to maintain the display boards with interesting topics, news headlines, puzzles and stuff like that. In recess, that area was always crowded as the whole school came to check. One such day while Laxmi was checking the board reading an article written by their classmate she took hold of her friend's hand and started discussing about the article. After a while she realized her friend was not responding back and that the hands felt a little hard. As she looked, next to her she was shocked to see that she was holding on to the head boy's hand all the while nicely chatting with him imagining him to be her friend. The whole of hallway became aware of the situation making it very awkward for Laxmi. The head boy looked equally shocked staring at her. Laxmi not knowing how to react to the situation started looking for her friends in the hallway. She saw her friends standing at the exit door with weird expressions. Hastily she removed her hands from his said sorry running towards her friends. Everybody left the room silently but as they neared their classes Poonam burst out laughing to which all of them started laughing loudly teasing Laxmi. She was so embarrassed about the whole situation but looking at them laugh she joined them laughing which gave her relief. Then onwards they started teasing Laxmi with his name which was irritating to her. In the same week Laxmi came little late to the school, her classmate from the group was waiting for her in the class not joining the class line for assembly. Laxmi hurriedly kept her bag and both left for the ground to join prayers, but by the time they went prayer had already started to which both got frightened not knowing what to do? They headed back to their class. During assembly classrooms were checked weather students are bunking the prayers. For their luck that day head boy came for checking found them in the class. Laxmi had already met him before and not in a good circumstance, as that day even he was with group of boys who were laughing at him. Today as he was coming towards them, they were too scared not knowing how he would take it up. Standing right in front of Laxmi, he asked them the reason for not attending assembly. Her friend said she's having stomach ache whereas Laxmi said she was late for school today so couldn't join. They looked at each other shocked knowing they were in big trouble. He looked angrily at them questioning were they lying? With lot of courage Laxmi spoke again, said she was late as she entered the class room, she saw her friend sitting at her desk complaining of stomach pain, so they both stayed back. He asked Laxmi to write a letter stating she was late for school today that it won't happen again. Laxmi immediately penned downed the letter and gave it to him. He asked Laxmi should he punish her or make her stand in front of principal's office as late comers had to go through that process. Laxmi with her big eyes kept staring at him with fear not knowing what to answer? She could hear his voice vaguely, concentrating more she heard him say, fine as it was Laxmi's first time, he would spare her for this time and started leaving the room. Before leaving he turned back and Laxmi could see a funny smile on his face as if he was teasing her. Both the friends looked at each other with relief. The whole day this was the ongoing topic in the group. Teasing turned into Laxmi being head boy's crush. Laxmi reacted back to them saying it's all due to the novels they were reading forming such ideas. Then the girls started digging head boy's background. His name was Sandeep, quite a handsome looking boy. He was the topper of the school and very active in sports too. He was the whole school's crush and was living in the hostel. While this was the hot topic in the group Meera announced that next week it was her brother's birthday and that everyone had to attend as she was informing beforehand to be prepared. Laxmi asked where would be the celebrations? Meera said it was kind of double celebrations, as her brother also finished training and was joining forces. So, he planned to host it at home to be able to invite his colony as well as school friends. Meera finished by saying it would be great fun as her brothers' an awesome host. All the girls agreed. It was easy for them as they were all from the same colony only Laxmi was a civilian. Laxmi said she had to take her parent's permission after which she would confirm. Everybody started to discuss what they would be wearing on that day Laxmi was happy as the topic got diverted.

In the evening when Laxmi's father came home from work and she asked for his permission to attend the birthday party. Surprisingly he agreed on a condition that she has to be back home at 8 o' clock and that he would arrange a car to be gone along with her. Laxmi thanked her father promising him that she will stick to the time. Next day in school she told her friends that she got permission to attend the party.

Within no time the day came for the party. Laxmi started from her home to Meera's place. By reaching the main gate of the colony security allowed the vehicle to pass by as Meera had taken the gate pass for Laxmi informing the guards her purpose of visit. As the car entered the colony it reminded Lamxi of the colony they used to live in with little difference in the setup. Meera had shared the bungalow number making it easy for Laxmi to trace. As she got near to the house Laxmi saw all new faces wondering how's it going to be? As she entered Meera came welcoming her, thanking her to be on time leading towards their friends. Laxmi was wearing a beige knee length frock with a beautiful belt, which her father had bought from London. Everybody complimented her at the choice of her dress and that she was looking very beautiful. Once the mutual admiration was done Laxmi started looking around and asked Meera where her parents were as she wanted to greet them. Meera smiled at Laxmi telling her it's all kids as her parents wanted them to have their own space also to enjoy the moment. Laxmi was astonished to hear that at the same time thinking such open-minded parents they were. More people joined; party games started with loud music being played all the while. English music was being played, which Laxmi was not exposed much but she enjoyed it a lot. Such a fun ambience was created while snacks kept on coming. Laxmi saw Meera's brother whispering something in Meera's ear wondering what they were sharing. After which Meera directly came to them dragging all to a corner. Wickedly she spread her hands, which had a cigarette packet and a lighter. Excitedly she said let's try what say? Continuing she said that my brother gave it to me for us girls to have an experience.

Everybody shared a glimpse of each other not knowing how to react as none of the girls were prepared for this! As the silence was killing her, Laxmi spoke first sharing once she along with her sister had tried her father's cigarette and didn't mind trying it again. She pulled one from the case looked around, rest of the girls followed her. Everyone lit the cigarettes smoking together giggling a lot. Suddenly Meera's brother peeped in shouting, 'enjoy girls.'

Laxmi felt time flew so fast already it was time for her to leave. She was the first among her friends to say bye to everybody, wishing the brother birthday again also congratulating on his achievements. Going back home

Laxmi thought would anybody find out about her smoking cigarette? By the time she reached home it was dinner time so everybody was preoccupied. She thanked God. Sharing how well the party was organized with others' she finished her dinner heading to her room.

An evening Laxmi was sitting on her study desk finishing her school work she heard her father calling her. Taking break from her work she went to the main balcony where he was sitting with his friend enjoying his evening tea. They both looked at her, asked what was she doing? Laxmi replied saying she was finishing her school work. Then they asked her, how was her new school? Has she settled down well? Made friend? Few other general questions. Though she was answering them not understanding where the conversation was heading? Uncle put forth a few more questions about studies, than asked her if she can speak for continuously five minutes in English if he gave her any random topic? Laxmi said she had never done so before but she would definitely try. Her uncle picked a topic about climate. Laxmi took a couple of seconds made points in her mind and started talking about climate in English. While delivering her speech she looked at her father who looked proud of his daughter's skills. Everything she learned at school, read in newspapers, magazines observing her surroundings all of which came handy for Laxmi to speak about the topic. They checked with her of her availability of time, asking her to talk on couple of more topics enjoying her view point. Sharing with her that she has a different take on all the topics, which is a good quality, suggesting her to always have it intact in any given situation. They then asked her to finish her balance school work. Laxmi was very happy with herself, being able to speak on the assigned topics in fluent English as it was a language she was learning in school. Next day after coming from school she again went to the same balcony spend some time there. Before that she had never enjoyed the space, standing at the rail of balcony she saw that their house was located right at the intersection of four road giving good view of the colony also good spot for time pass. She could see people walking, vehicles going by, kids playing more such activities. While she was watching saw two dogs fighting a man hushing them away, then she heard loud sound of motorbikes coming in very high speed. She was standing right at the intersection roads on a height, Laxmi saw two bike riders ridding on two adjacent roads heading towards the intersection. The riders were speeding so fast, before she could anticipate the moment both the bikes collided with each other. The impact was so bad one of the riders flew high in the air falling down on ground. The sound was so loud that people around also from inside the house came out to see what was the cause of the sound. All went running to the spot to help the riders. Laxmi scared looking at it, ran inside the house to tell her brother what happened outside. Listening to her, her brother asked has she seen their faces? Are they from the colony? She told him riders looked young were not wearing helmets also saw the face of the boy who flew in the air but she had never seen them before. Laxmi's brother hurriedly ran out to help them wanting to find out what happened? Who was involved in the accident? Laxmi waited for her brother to return soon to know more about the situation, as she was not able to forget the episode. After a while he came back, told them boys were juniors from his college that luckily nobody was injured. They bought new bikes were having fun going around which backfired by colliding into each other. Laxmi thought what kind of fun was it stupidly speeding risking lives without any safety measures taken.

Few days later Laxmi was sitting in the balcony chitchatting with her grandmother. While doing so her grandmother pointing towards a boy on road asking was, he the same boy who met with accidents in front of their house? Laxmi looked at where she was pointing to see a boy wearing shorts with bandages on his legs and hands carrying some groceries limping while walking. At close counter she could recollect his face, kept staring to confirm firmly. Suddenly the boy looked at Laxmi, hastily she looked away from him cursing herself to be in such awkward position. The boy causally waved at her with a smile while kept walking away from them. After seeing such a dreadful accident Laxmi pictured the victims in very worst situation, nothing like the one which she was happening in front of her. It was so funny Laxmi burst out laughing at both extremes. Grandmother tried to silence her telling her not to laugh on anyone that way taking her inside the house. She narrated the whole incident at home, which everyone felt funny laughing it loud. Though her grandmother was teaching manners to all Laxmi saw her grandmother also smiling leaving the room. Her brother shared more saying the boys had become the talk of the colony after the accident. Making people wonder how even they survived, the fall being from such height. Laxmi developed little familiarity with the boy whenever they came across in the colony exchanging smiles.

The house was not as big as the one in pervious colony, they had to share rooms about that even bathrooms. Mainly in winters it was mad rush hour at home while getting ready for school. Getting in first in restrooms would have the luxury of steaming hot water, latter had to adjust to warm water for bathing. Laxmi's father would wake up in little late than kids for his office. His rooms bathroom was available, being in line Laxmi's sister would slowly tuck herself in their father's bed to catchup on sleep. Daily their mother had to drag her out pushing her into bathroom. Laxmi's father's bedroom had an attached balcony, which was kept closed most of the mornings. That day for some reason the balcony door was left semi open, nobody paid attention concentrating much on getting ready. Laxmi's mother asked her to wake her sister besides her father as she was running late preparing breakfast and tiffin boxes. Amidst of her getting ready Laxmi went near her father's bed. She saw two bundles under the blanket assuming bigger one being her father she headed towards the other side of the bed.

As she approached towards the bed, she heard her sister calling her asking her to get ready fast as they were getting late. Her sister entered the room, looking at each other both of them stared at the small bump under the blanket. Thinking who has taken her place out of curiosity Laxmi moved the blanket. To her surprise she saw a small monkey sleeping next to Laxmi's father nicely tucked under the blanket. Looking at her the monkey shouted jumping towards the balcony door, frightened Laxmi shouted continued by her sister waking up their father horrified. Before anybody could react, the monkey sneaked out of the door. As the balcony door opened there was whole families of monkey's sitting!! God knows doing what? Their father was next to the door reacted fast closing the door immediately stopping more monkeys from coming in. Then he said all's fine, asked the kids to get ready for school as they were getting late. All the while riding cycle to school Laxmi and her sister kept on talking about monkey's laughing along. After coming from school, the topic still continued at home, teasing their father having a new child in the family. To which he joked back saying the new sibling has some resemblance to Laxmi.

Chapter 8
High School

As years passed by, Laxmi had entered class tenth in school. In Indian education system, it's considered to be an important milestone to climb. It was very serious at home as well, as the same year her brother was appearing for class 12th final exams. The most important difference being that usually in all the classes the teachers who teaches, prepares the question paper also corrects the paper. But these two years question paper is set by different teacher, corrected by some other teacher finally taught by another teacher so the student has to cater to different teachers while preparing and writing exams which is tough.

One of these days while Laxmi was going home along with her friends and crossing the ground towards the cycle stand, she heard her name being called from behind. Laxmi turned back to see the head boy waving at her to which she looked at her friends and they all had that teasing smile on their faces. Before she could say anything to her friends Sandeep the head boy was standing right in front of her. Astonished she looked at him! Understanding the under current in the situation he smiled at her asking why her brother didn't come to school today? Laxmi replied back saying he had a fever so he couldn't attend school. He asked to convey the message from the class teacher that very important classes were being held. Not to miss classes, passing a slip to give to her brother asking him to come prepared for next day along with the topics covered today, and saying so he waved goodbye and left. Going to school all siblings went together, coming back from school everyone rode with friends as their timings were different. On the way back it was difficult for her to stop her friends from giggling and teasing. Finally, she decided to ditch the gang for the day racing ahead of them all. Splitting from the group she reached home and upon entering the house she directly went to her brother's room to share the information, which was passed to her. To her utter surprise she saw the head boy sitting next to her brother chatting coolly. Looking at Laxmi with snobbish expression he said hostel warden had sent him to fetch a few things, on the way back he was visiting his friend as he was not well. Once again, she was relieved none of her friends saw what she was seeing. Handing over the slip to Sandeep and giving him one serious look left the room without further discussion. After a while when Sandeep was leaving and he met Laxmi in the living room, she didn't know what to say to which he again spoke teasingly asking her how were her friend's doing? Did she enjoy her friend's birthday party? These questions made Laxmi wonder how he knew about the party! Before she could say anything else he left. To which her brother came back and asked what was he saying. Laxmi got hold of herself not knowing what to say, recollected the whole situation nd telling him that Sandeep had met at school given her the slip shared what the class teacher had said. Laxmi's brother very casually brushed it aside saying he knew about it at the same time giving her mischievous looks to which Laxmi asked what!

Nothing

Finally, the day of board exams came. As Laxmi was getting ready her father said not to worry and that he will drop her to the school. It was a big relief as the stress was really high. They both got into the car, and as the car was coming out of the gate the bike crash guy (bikey) they named him came in front of the car and gave a smile almost like wishing her good luck for exams, Laxmi smiled back forgetting her father was sitting right next to her. Expecting her father not to observe she started praying to God. As she opened her eyes the first thing her father asked was does she know the boy? She replied back. Not personally she doesn't know him, but he's the same guy who met accident in front of their house about whom she had told him before. He was convinced with her answer and further asked her to concentrate on exam.

Laxmi's father dropped her wishing her good luck. Told her that he'll come back to pick her up and to stand where he left her. As she entered the school, she met her friends discussed the topics, later everyone dispersed to their assigned classrooms. In the classroom the desks were marked with roll numbers. Laxmi looked for hers and settled down. Bell rang, everyone was waiting for teachers to come. Each class was assigned two teachers. First teacher came, greeted and started sharing instructions when the second teacher entered the classroom. Laxmi looked at the teacher immediately recollecting from previous school. He was transferred from the school by her father, as the teacher was misbehaving with girl students and Laxmi's sister had bought the situation to notice by informing her father. In those days, a lot of tension had prevailed. As the school came under Laxmi's father's management, he had to handle the matter carefully. Instead of banning from teaching which all the parents wanted. He got him transferred to another branch without spoiling his career. Asked the teacher to apologise to the management and parents leaving the campus. So, Laxmi was scared looking at the teacher of his reputation not knowing what he might be up to now? The papers were distributed, students started attempting the question paper. After a while the teacher came and stood next to her. Laxmi gave a smile to him wishing him good morning. He bowed back but stood there while reading her answer. Not knowing what to do she nervously kept writing her paper. Slowly he pointed some mistakes helping her in answering paper, even though the other teacher was looking along with students. By the time she finished rest of her paper submitted it. Looked around for sir to talk to him thanking him, he was gone. As the time was ticking her father would be waiting, she left the school hurriedly. He asked her how did she attempt the paper? Laxmi told him it was not a tough paper and that she performed fairly fine. Laxmi also told him about the teacher, that he helped him with few answers also before she could thank him, he left the classroom and she couldn't meet him. Laxmi's father heard her asked her to forget the incident focusing on the next paper.

The days went by so fast and in no time, Laxmi finished exams while her brother finished a week later. After which they had to wait a long one whole month for their results to be announced. To keep her occupied, Laxmi joined hobby classes that too wounded up in no time making everybody wait for the results eagerly. As the day of results came Laxmi prayed to God before leaving for school. There was mad rush at the display board. 12th class exam results were also displayed. Laxmi thought she did well and proceeded to check her brother's result too. He had scored perfect (100/100) in both maths as well as physics, placing himself in the merit list. She was so proud of her brother as she could never accomplish something like that. Hurriedly she went to her class to collect her marksheet. Though she passed in first class but was not in the merit list. Still, she was happy of her achievement, along with her all her friends too had passed in first class.

But before coming to school her father had shared that he had again been transferred to a place near Calcutta. Laxmi was very sad as she had to again change schools and make new friends. She was enjoying the town life so much and again they had to move to a little township. Laxmi shared the news with her friends. To her surprise couple of her friends father's too got transferred to different places, they were also shifting in the holidays. They all promised to be in touch through letters and never discontinue writing.

After reaching home she congratulated her brother from that the discussion led to where he would continue his study as the place where they were moving to couldn't support college studies. He appeared for many entrance exams and got admission in a top private engineering college in the same town. Once the admission process was finished along with his hostel admission the family left for the township. Laxmi' father had to take charge of his duties, also to settle other kids in their respective classes.

The shifting happened like last time. Laxmi got her own room like before, only difference being she was not as excited like the first time she had been . She was missing her school, friends, home where she was living even more her brother. By evening Laxmi's father came home, asked them to be ready next day, as he would take them to join the new school.

Next day their father took them to the new school and got them admitted to their respective classes before leaving. . Laxmi was escorted to her class. This school was half the size of her earlier school, which had only one section of her class and also one third of the class strength than the previous one. The school children looked entirely different so she requested her mother to pick her up and drop daily from school. It looked quite awkward for a high school girl to be tagging along with her mother. One day a teacher asked Laxmi's mother why she was taking all the trouble, while the school was inside the colony. It was a walkable distance in the colony so most of the kids walked to school. The teacher assured her mother that she will take care of Laxmi asking her to commute independently. Slowly she made friends and started getting adjusted to the new environment. As the day passed by, activities in the school started. Laxmi was designated as the house captain as not many students were there in the school. House teacher had put her name in all activities. Looking at the long list of events she requested the teacher to take off her name from few activities. He said he would do so if Laxmi could replace with any other student. She was quite new and didn't know much of the students, hence she had to oblige to the teacher participating in all the activities he had enrolled her. Playing sports was easy as most of them were played in groups. Rugby was a new game to her as she had never played it before. . Teacher didn't know that Laxmi was clueless about the game and and neither did Laxmi until she entered the ground seeing kids holding the ball in hands running. Even the shape of the ball she was seeing for the first time. Hurriedly she ran to the teacher and told her plight, he looked more confused at the last minute asking her to join the team and play. As the house teacher was not from a sports background, he couldn't help her explaining the game laughing at her situation she headed towards the boys house captain to explain the game. In such short time he could only share basic structure along with rules of the game. The least he could do was guide her mid of game if she needed assistance from far. She being the captain couldn't contribute much but luckily her team was very strong and finally they won the game.

The sports activities section was finished with this game. Laxmi bought laurels to her house by winning carrom board, and table tennis playing all by herself. Teacher was very happy and impressed by her. The other competitions related to co-curricular activities were announced. She was assigned to participate in the elocution competition. They shared the topic asked them to prepare the speech and get ready. Laxmi went through lot of books, magazines but couldn't write a decent high school stuff. Not understanding what to do? Roaming around the house when her eyes got fixed on the telephone. Laxmi got an idea call her father's office. Laxmi's father's personal assistant picked the phone as usual. She spoke to him asking where her father was? As her father would never entertain anything like this. The assistant told he was in a meeting won't be available for couple of hours. She was thrilled thought this was her moment. Told him (PA) she had to participate in elocution competition and needed someone to write speech for her on the given topic while also requesting him not let her father to know about it. In no time he wrote a powerful speech, sent it through the office peon.

Major part of the issue was sorted out but now came her turn to memorize the whole speech. Laxmi thoroughly memorized the speech, practiced before the mirror many times, recorded her speech in a recorder heard her speech many times. Putting total efforts from her side. Keeping in mind her teacher whom she didn't want to disappoint. Finally, the day came. One by one everybody's turn was finished, then came Laxmi's turn. One of her classmates was also participating from another house. He finished before her Laxmi thought that he was quite good at it that and she had to outperform him, if she had to win the competition. As she was thoroughly prepared, she went on the stage confidently and greeted everybody before starting the speech. She was doing an excellent job nearing to competition of the speech, when all of the sudden a kid in the front row shouted disturbing the whole room. Even Laxmi got disturbed, distracted she got confused forgetting few lines she couldn't finish the speech as effectively as she began. She was very disappointed by her performance, which resulted in her to settle for second prize.

Chapter 9
Mela (fete)

Laxmi's father's boss was a nice man who frequently visited them along with his wife, unfortunately he didn't have any kids. He was native to a nearby town from where her father also hailed from. There was a very nice bond developed between the families. They would look upon Laxmi and her siblings very affectionately and spend a lot of time with their family. While having dinner on a weekend, the topic about travelling came up where everybody shared their experiences. Suddenly Mr. Rajan (boss) remembered that during this month in a nearby lake migratory birds came from different continent. They should plan one outing as it would be good exposure to kids along with a fun learning activity. Mr. Rajan further said that he would find more information about the place for visiting there next weekend.

Next day Laxmi went to school all thrilled imagining the next weekend and thinking of spending time together along with the extended family. The week passed by very quickly in making arrangements for the travel. It was just a day trip; they would be back by dinner. They planned three cars one each for elders, kids & staff. They started at dawn to reach back for dinner, which was planned at the guest house. First break they took for coffee and breakfast. The staff arranged quite a neat picnic for the families . The sandwiches, cutlets, biscuits tasted tastier than usual along with the beverages. As the journey continued Laxmi observed that they passed the villages and almost every home had a small pond planned in front of their houses.

Later during a small break, she mentioned it to her father. Mr. Rajan came by and said very good observation. As fish being their staple food included in daily diet, they all maintain those ponds to grow fishes and use it while cooking. It's like fish farming to which he nodded with a smile said 'yeah' you can say so. Fish farming was quiet fascinating for Laxmi reminding her of rearing chicken in the backyard by her mother. Similarly, instead of chicken they were farming fishes, very interesting. Ultimately, they reached their destination. It was almost lunch time; they had to walk a small distance as cars couldn't go inside. Elders summoned the staff to arrange lunch by the time they came back from the lake visit.

As they walked along a small forest, they could see the lake from far with a huge gate and a watchman standing by. They spoke to the guard informing that they had come to watch the migratory birds. Laxmi read the board where some instructions were given strictly prohibiting from feeding the birds as the natural ecosystem would be disturbed. The guard showed them a tower pointing them to take that particular route which would lead them to the tower. All of them followed the route and reached the tower. From the tower as they viewed the lake, it was a spectacular view. The lake was quite bigger than what Laxmi had imagined and also, she had never seen so many similar kind of birds together at the same time. The whole lake was filled with all sizes of birds and the water was totally covered. They were peculiar kind of birds, pinkish in color with long beaks which she had not seen anywhere. Mr. Rajan said they travel miles together without any break coming to this pond exactly in the same season every year. They make babies, stay for three months after which head to where they came from. It was astonishing to see how they travel without any maps or compass. Their minds are also comparatively very small in size and still the way they navigate is interesting maintaining the time as well. Their journey turned out to be very interesting, informative and knowledgeable too. Laxmi thanked Mr. Rajan for the wonderful experience. After spending quality time watching birds they headed back to the cars. By now everyone was very hungry as even the long walk added up. The staff picked a nice shaded place arranging hot (food) lunch in the middle of nowhere. They all enjoyed the lunch, thanked the staff for lovely lunch meanwhile kids helped the staff in sorting things arranging it back in car.

Their journey back started but as they had started quite early in the morning, they could make it back by evening tea time. Directly they went to the guest house. It was situated at the banks of river Ganges as the sun was setting and had a beautiful view. The river was flowing with small currents while the sun had spread the sky with smooth vivid colors. High tea along with snacks & pakodas was arranged, they spend some time chit chatting in the garden till it became quite dark. Until the dinner was being cooked, all of them played card games and once the dinner was ready., they enjoyed the spread and called it a day. While having dinner Laxmi's mom and Mrs. Rajan shared with them that the next month ladies club was organizing annual day celebrations. They had lined up a few cultural activities, competitions along with fete. They both were the main organizers and they were having a stall for dosas and vadas together. all the kids were asked to actively participate in all the activities.

As the next month arrived the whole colony was waiting for the events to start. They planned the whole week with one event a day. Ended up the event by organizing a fete. Wherein all the ladies had different stalls from where one can buy from them. They showcased fashionable clothes, jewelry, food stall, articles and many more. Amongst which the games stalls were handed over to young trainees who had joined the company freshly. These trainees were young graduates who finished college and joined the company. Laxmi got dressed for the evening along with her sister and then they left for the fete. they met rest of their friends and as planned visited all the stalls. Laxmi realized she was not carrying any money, so she headed straight to her mom's stall. She saw her mom very busy organizing the stall instructing the staff getting things done. Laxmi asked aren't you little late as people have already started coming, her mom said not to worry as everything was on time. Laxmi was relieved hearing her, took money and left to visit rest of the stalls. Going around they shopped for a few things, ate a lot of food and finally decided to play a few games. As they approached that section, they crossed other classmates who told them some interesting games which were there to play. Hence, they decided to play all the games one after another. As they started playing, they lost two games and went to try the third one. It was Laxmi's turn this time. The game had a huge board with a human figure on it labelling the body parts with the amount assigned. All one had to do was touch any body part and win the amount.

They would blindfold the contestant and cover the distance in ten steps, touch the body party winning the amount displayed. They thought it was quite easy forming a plan not to lose this game at least. They planned that Laxmi would be blindfolded while from the back the rest of the team would instruct right & left leading her to the board winning easily. Enthusiastically they all wanted to win this game anyhow also to earn some money too. As soon as Laxmi walked towards the board blindfolded, she was sure that their trick would work making her easily win. Following instructions, she started her walk, but suddenly mid of the game instructions stopped coming she could hear silence all around her. She didn't know what to do? She couldn't give up in between the game just like that, so she went ahead and kept on playing. As she walked ahead something came in contact with her hands. She thought she had reached that board and hurriedly started moving her hand to hit the jackpot (big amount). Suddenly it struck to her it didn't feel like board. Slowly she felt the object more feeling like some part of cloth between her fingers. Understanding something was wrong she pulled her blindfolded over her head astonished to see her hand on the chest of the trainee organizer who was equally surprised by the situation they were in. He didn't have the space to move as he was cornered to one end. Both looked at each other equally amused not able to decide what to do next as lot of people were watching them. Realizing the situation Laxmi said sorry to the guy running out of the place along with her friends. They stopped at a point laughing loudly looking at each other. Laxmi asked them why did they stop directing mid of the game leaving her like that. They informed her there was another person from the organizing team who instructed them not to direct Laxmi as it was considered cheating. They again laughed out loud, Laxmi could say nothing to them deciding not to play any more games. They wondered around for some more time eating some more food, as it was getting late and then left for their homes. Laxmi narrated the whole incident to her grandmother about what happened at fete. Her grandmother told her to stop being naughty to behave properly. Laxmi knew it just happened like that with nobody's fault in it but how to explain to her granny. Obediently said Okay went to her room. After freshening up before going to bed Laxmi couldn't forget the boy's expression on his face at the same time imagining how her expressions would have been laughing with smile on her face went to sleep.

Chapter 10

Parade

one sunny day, Laxmi and her sister were plucking vegetables from their kitchen garden, where the gardener Babu used to grow all kinds of fruits and vegetables according to the season. They plucked corn to roast and have it as a snack. Doing so Laxmi recollected that nobody was home that day, that they should do something exciting for fun. They thought for a while and Laxmi came up with a plan to drive the car all by themselves. Her sister didn't give much of a reaction, as they were very new to driving and still learning. Laxmi convinced her and asked her to sit beside her and she would take up the responsibility of driving. . Laxmi took the car keys and headed towards the garage. Her sister said that its quite dangerous what she was attempting to do and asked her to think twice. Laxmi said not to worry as it would be lot of fun. They opened the garage door as Laxmi slowly got the car outside, her sister opened the gate. As she bought the car outside her sister closed that gate getting into the car. As they started the mission both looked at each other and started giggling. Slowing Laxmi took a turn putting them on the main road. There was traffic which they hit, Laxmi got a little nervous while all sorts of ideas started cultivating in her head. Imagining hitting somebody on the road some passer by making everything going all wrong. Before the thoughts could engulf her, she decided to drive towards the sports stadium where it was less traffic, roads were broader. As they headed that way unexpectedly lot of vehicles were parked in the stadium with a lot of activities going on, it looked like some kind of event. As she had already taken a turn, she had no other way but to ride ahead. She was a beginner and this was her first solo drive without any instructor that's the reason Laxmi was being super conscious while driving. Going ahead she felt that she was seeing familiar faces but as she was concentrating on driving, didn't much gave a thought about it. Moving ahead she felt like seeing her father's driver, but waved off thinking they should be in office not near the stadium. Going ahead she saw her father standing with confused expression asking them to stop the car. Slowly Laxmi stopped the car and her father came near to Laxmi politely asking her whose idea was it? Laxmi's sister immediately pointed towards Laxmi saying she had nothing to do with it. In an undertone voice, he said who else could think of something like that. Rest of his colleagues started to gather and he immediately asked them to go home. Seeing all the people Laxmi got nervous but somehow managed to reverse the car and head home. Laxmi parked the car in garage, thrilled by her courageous driving experience. She thought of enjoying the moment as anyhow in the evening there was going to be a hot discussion about it after her father came from office. Her mom was home by then and gave very bad looks, going upstairs she said let your father handle the situation. In the evening when everyone was waiting for Mr. Venkat, for Laxmi the time felt like never ending. As he came called everyone to join him for tea. Asked Laxmi where does she get such an idea from? Laxmi though he looked happy rather than being angry so she opened up and shared her solo driving experience. Ya, my friends feel the same he said. Further, he said that apparently, they judged Laxmi as a very good driver . Then he said but that doesn't mean you attempt it again.

He explained the dangers, risks other problems associated to it, said once he approves of her, she could go solo driving. Laxmi apologized (said sorry) promised never to repeat the mistake than asked him what was he doing at the stadium as she was expecting him at office around that time. He replied back saying as it was Independence Day tomorrow as every year they were arranging the place for parade, activities, snacks for the community. Then he shared awesome news that as he was heading the company he was assigned to take the honor of salute on stage hence instructed none of them to miss the event.

The next day was such a rush as the parade started quite early they had to get ready leave for stadium. Mr. Venkat had already left by the time they got up so they had to hurry too.

Laxmi and her friends spotted a good spot and sat on the stadium chairs. After a few speeches, it was Laxmi's father turn, he delivered quite an impressive speech. Flew some doves in the sky and announced the parade to start. The guards marched passed Laxmi's father where he stood saluting the battalion as one after another followed. Laxmi felt so proud of her father and thought what her career would be like? After which national Anthem started everyone got up from their seats and paid respect. While taking her seat Laxmi saw, after two rows all the company trainees were seated, whom she saw on the fete day and thought that boy would be also among them. As Laxmi sat some girls came and introduced themselves saying they had also joined the company as trainees and were working under her father. In no time Laxmi made friends with them and asked how they were passing their time after office? Because Laxmi knew there was not much to do, so she invited them to the officer's club to spend some time along. They discussed lot of topics like what novels they were reading, then the boys walked in and asked to be introduced.

Everybody knew about the incident at the fete which they kept under wraps and finally introduced the guy. He was Sameer, he said hi and continued informing Laxmi & her friends that the next week they were assigned to coach higher class students in basketball and throw ball at their school. Asked if any of them were in the teams? They all nodded to which he said 'see you all on the playground then', said bye and left.

After that day, daily they would expect the trainees to turnup on the field but they never showed up. One day during recess while having lunch the peon came to the classroom and informed the whole class to meet the principal after the break. As the class stood at principal's office imagining all kinds of stuff, where they all had made mistakes again. Last time when the whole class decided to bunk the school on the same day they got warning from the principal as it was their final year of school and the extra classes were being conducted for them to perform better in exams. While scolding the class principal looked at Laxmi who had a smile on her face to which principal continued scolding more and informing that he's saying seriously and not take it lightly. Coming out of the principal office the whole class pointed at Laxmi blaming her but because of her smile it went more serious in the office. Incidentally Laxmi realized that's the expression she always carried smile, which always lead to similar situations.

Remembering that incident all were worried, as the door opened along with principal came the trainee boys whom Sir introduced as coaches also as they just passed out could also help preparing them for exams. The colony being in the interior place to find teachers for higher classes was getting a hassle so the management came with a solution to handle the situation.

It worked out quiet well as everybody got along fine and their guidance in preparing for exams helped the student well. Laxmi finished her school year that year looking forward for the next phase of the journey LIFE.

Hope you enjoyed the novel…. spare us for grammatical and printing errors.

Hi,

Reader's

I have planned a small contest in the book, please participate. The main idea to be able to develop correspondence between us. In the contest try to figure out from which chapter the illustration belong along with page number. Write review about the book email us at: biorhythmthroughlife@gmail.com

The first 25 contestants will receive gift hampers

Have an elegant mind to build a holistic lifestyle

www.ingramcontent.com/pod-product-compliance
Lightning Source LLC
LaVergne TN
LVHW041538070526
838199LV00046B/1733